A GOLDEN BOOK · NEW YORK

ISBN 978-0-593-37375-0 (trade)

rhcbooks.com

Printed in the United States of America

10 9 8 7 6 5 4 3 2 1

2021 Edition

Oh, no! Mayor Humdinger has moved to Adventure City, and now he's the mayor.

Using the top picture as a guide, can you draw him on the bottom grid?

Help the PAW Patrol find their way to Adventure City so they can save the people from the mayor's silly plans.

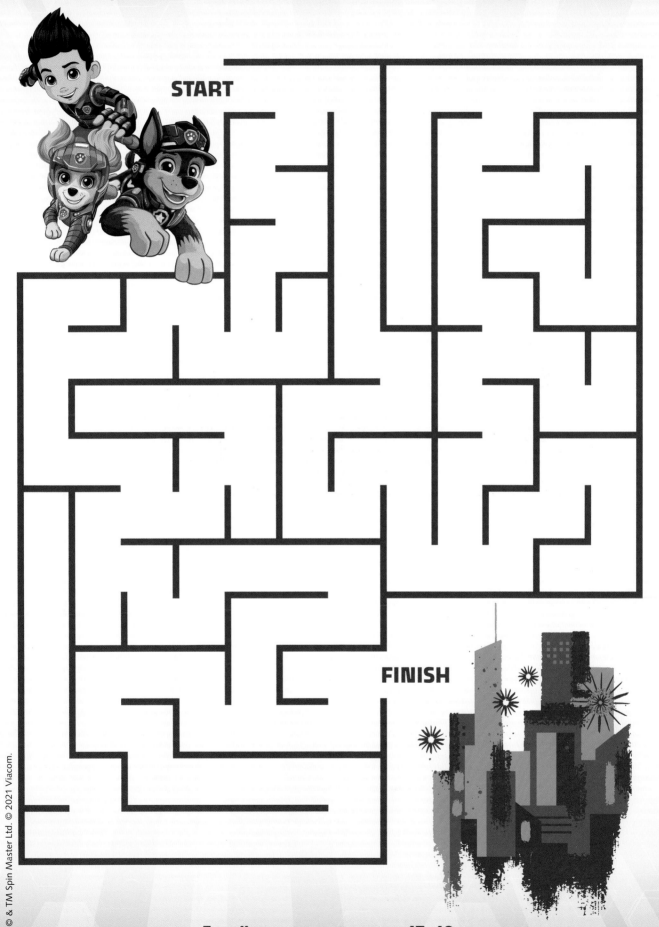

START

FINISH

For all answers, see pages 47–48.

Adventure City is big, and there are so many things to see.

Study the picture below, then look at the next page and see if you can spot four differences there.

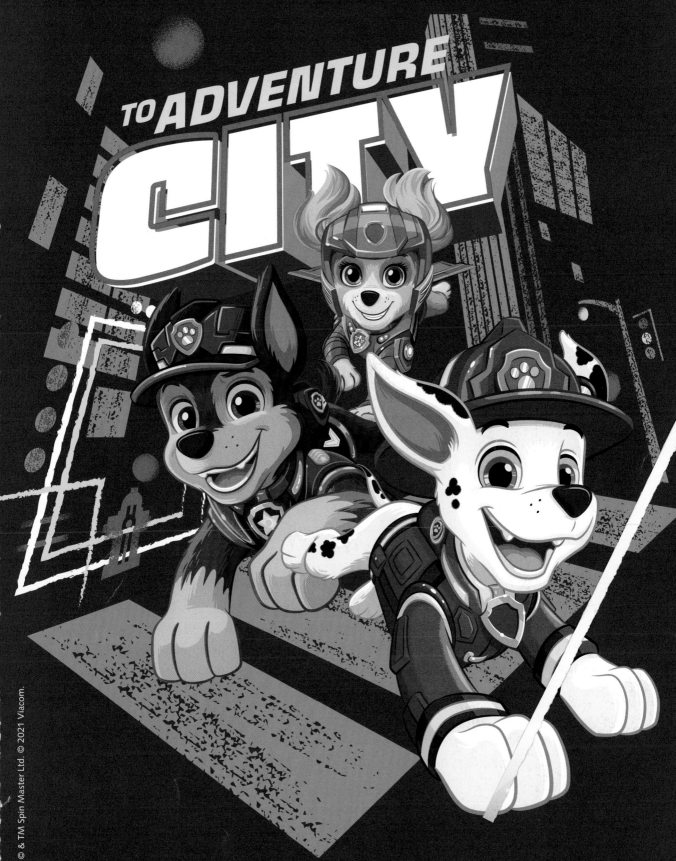

LIBERTY

Liberty lives in Adventure City and loves the PAW Patrol.

Can you find the t___ ___s of her that match?

Mayor Humdinger wants to make a big bang in Adventure City.

Can you draw some fireworks for him?

SKYE

Color this picture of Skye and Liberty!

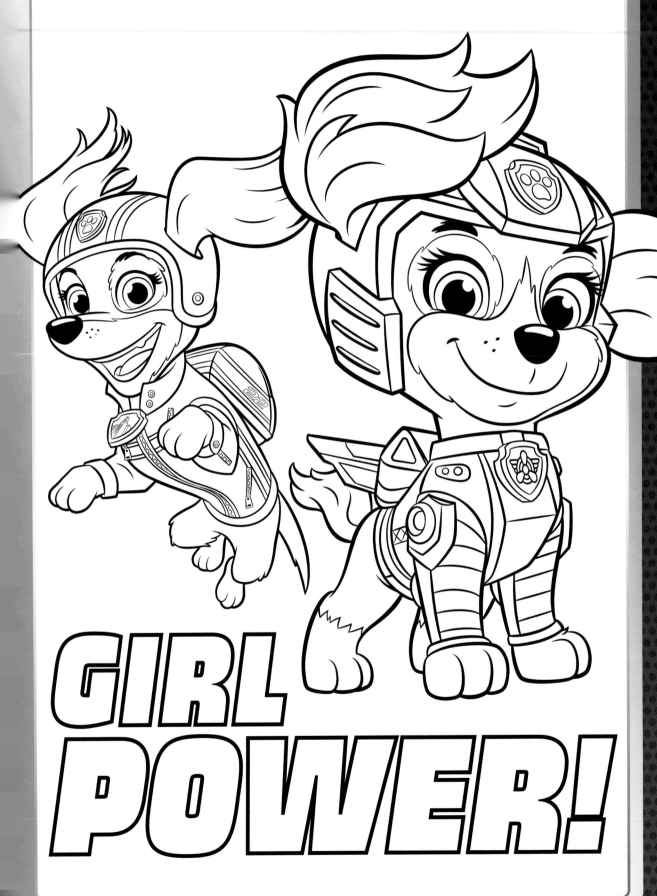

Terrific Treats!

The PAW Patrol has new headquarters in Adventure City—and Rubble really likes the treat machine! With a friend, take turns drawing a line to connect two dots. If a line you draw completes a box, give yourself a point. If your box contains a treat, give yourself two points. Whoever has more points after all the boxes have been completed wins.

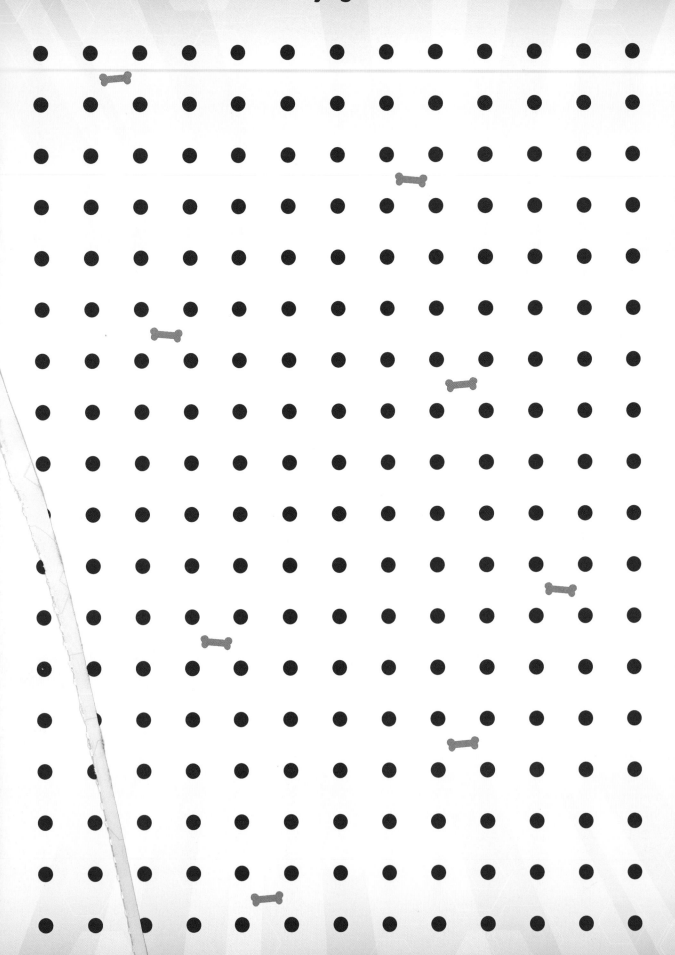

RUBBLE

Using the top picture as a guide, finish the bottom picture of Rubble.

Have a grown-up help you cut out this sign for your door.

THIS PUP IS HOME!

© & TM Spin Master Ltd. © 2021 Viacom.

THIS PUP IS
ON A
MISSION!

When Chase was little, he got lost in Adventure City.

Can you help him find his way to Ryder?

START

FINISH

19

CHASE

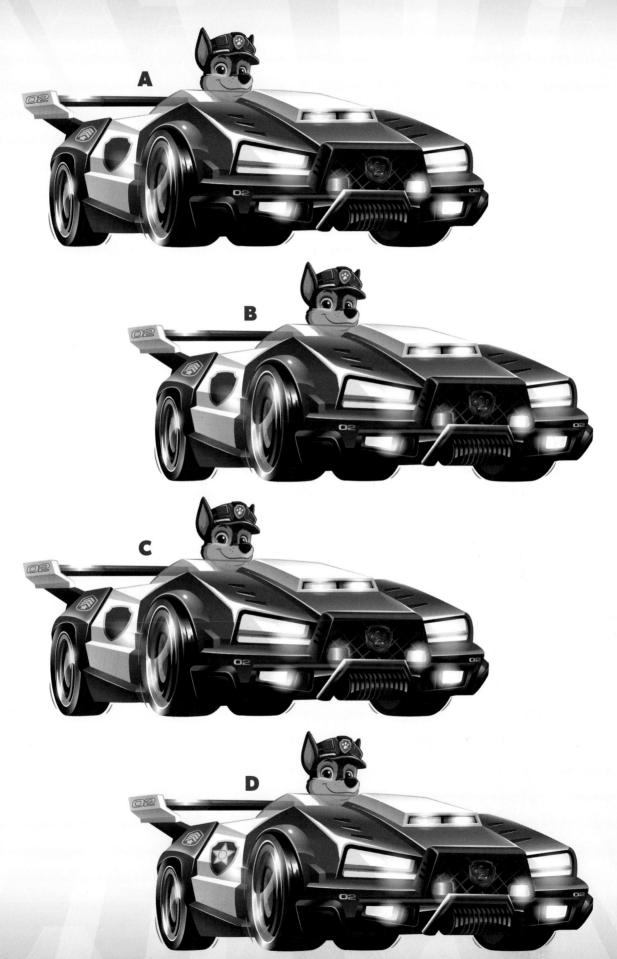

Chase has been captured by a dogcatcher and taken to the pound. Can the team save him?

Using the smaller picture as a guide,
color Ryder and Liberty.

SAVE CHASE!

(For two players)

Carefully remove this page from the book and place it on the floor. Take turns with a friend flipping a coin onto the game board. If your coin touches a picture, you get the number of points listed. The first player to land on Chase AND reach ten points wins!

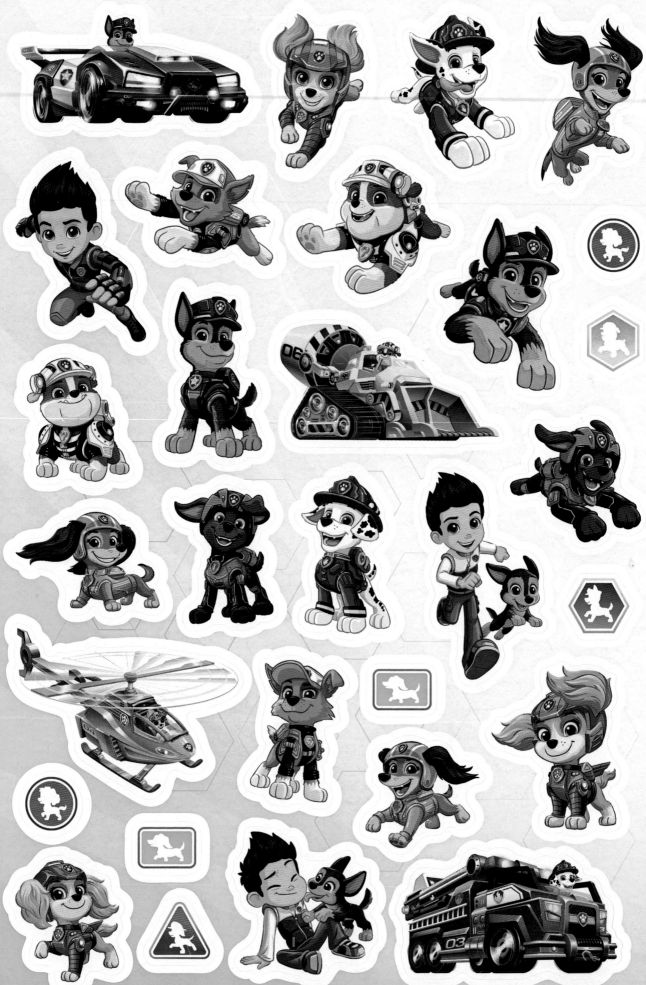

RYDER

Mayor Humdinger's weather machine is out of control.

With a friend, start the mazes on this page and the next at the same time and see who can race to the rescue first!

START

FINISH

FINISH

START

Liberty and Rubble to the rescue!

Help them find the path to Chase and the pound.

START

FINISH

ROCKY

Use your stickers to create a scene that shows the PAW Patrol ready to save the day!

ZUMA

Liberty wants to help the team!
Can you find the path that will lead her to them?

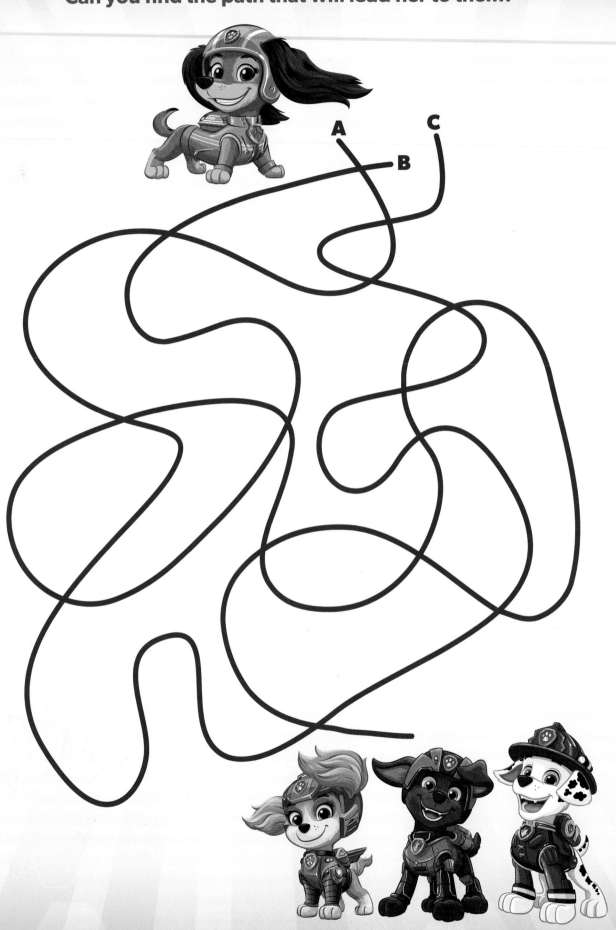

A

B

C

LITTLE PUPS CAN DO BIG THINGS!

Can you match each PAW Patrol team member here to their close-up pictures on the next page?

Cheer for the pups!

How many times can you find the word PAW in the puzzle?
Look up, down, backward, and forward.

P P A W W W
P A W P A A
P P P W A P
W P A A W P
A A W P P A
P W P W A P

Draw yourself with the PAW Patrol!

MAKE A GIANT PAW PATROL POSTER!

- Carefully remove the next four pages and trim the edges.
- Lay them facedown in the correct order.
- Tape the pages together and hang the poster on your wall!

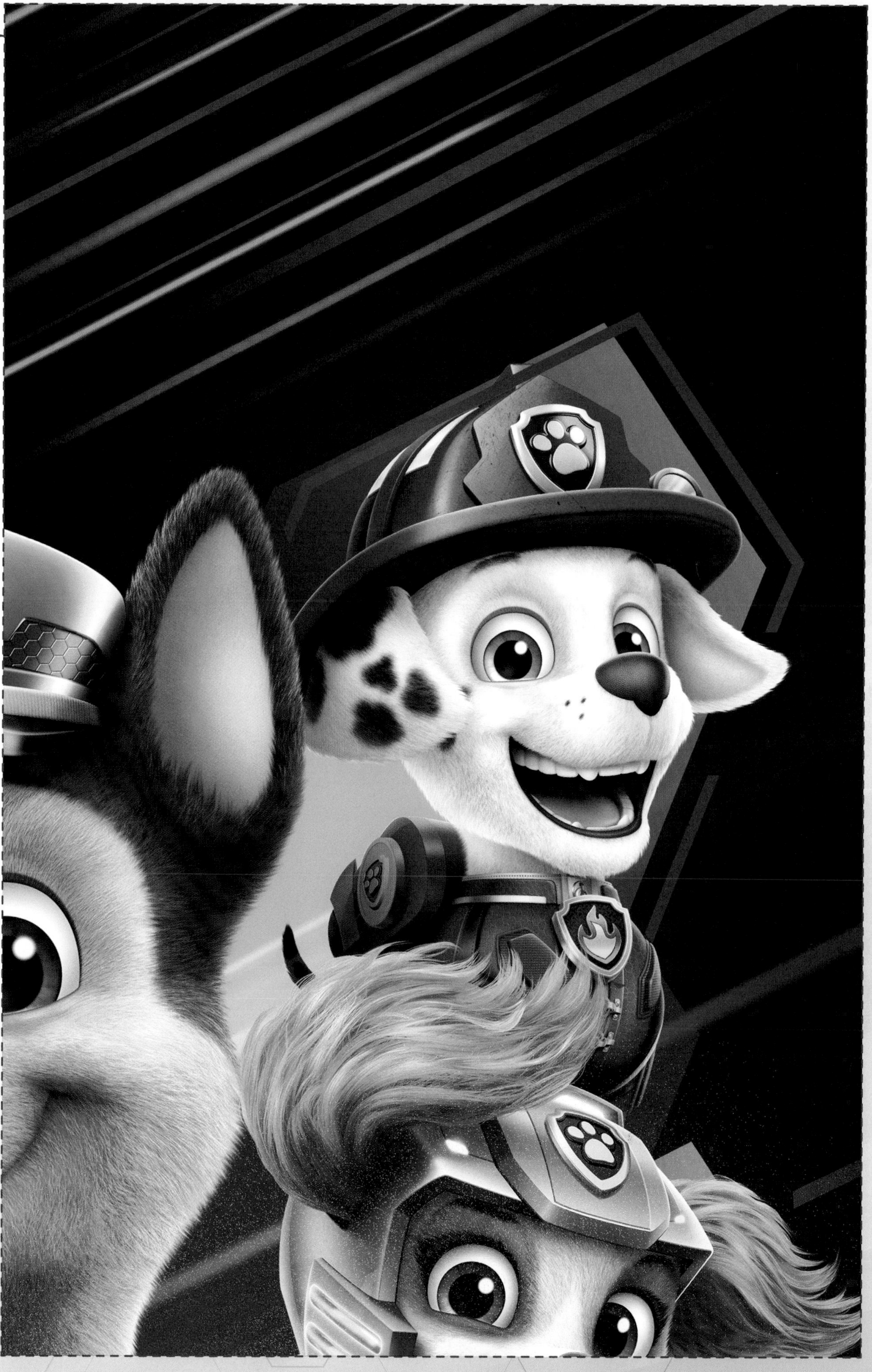

nickelodeon